The Best ME That I Can Be

HONESTY

BY ROSE ANGEBRANDT

Published and written by Rose Angebrandt

ISBN: 978-1-9991187-3-0

Copyright © 2019 by Rose Angebrandt

www.roseangebrandt.com

For Keigan and Ayzlin

You are loved more than words can say

My name is Ayzlin. I want to be

the best *me* that I can be!

To be the best *me* that I can be I should always try my very best to be honest. This means telling the truth and doing what I know is right and not doing things that I know are wrong.

But sometimes things just happen that can make

being honest very hard. Mommy always tells me

not to play near her very favorite flowers.

I was so busy seeing how fast I could spin

that I spun right into the flower garden.

I spun so fast that I fell on top of Mommy's very favorite flowers and broke them.

Mommy works so hard to make her flower garden beautiful.

It doesn't look very nice right now. I think I'm going to be in big trouble. Oh No! What am I going to do? This is not good. Mommy's very favorite flowers are badly broken!

Hey! I know! I'll tell Mommy that Rosco did it! I'll say he was rolling and digging on top of her very favorite flowers. I could see he was breaking them. I tried to call him but he wouldn't come and that's how they got really broken.

But... then Mommy will be mad at Rosco and he will be in big trouble for something he didn't do.

That would not be a nice thing for me to do to Rosco. That would not be honest. Rosco is my best friend.

I know! I'll tell Mommy it was Bobby from down the street. He is always in trouble and doing things he shouldn't be doing. I'll say he just ran into the flower garden and started jumping on Mommy's very favorite flowers for no reason! I saw he was breaking them and yelled at him to stop but he kept on jumping. That's why they are really badly broken.

But... then Mommy will call his Mommy to "talk about it".
Bobby will be in big trouble... for something he didn't do.

That would not be a very nice thing for me to do. That
would not be honest... even if Bobby is always in trouble.

What if I tell Mommy that I just don't know what

happened to her very favorite flowers.

"Mommy....maybe it was some dancing baby goats?"...

"Mommy, I think I've seen giant rolling

turtles in the flower garden before"...

"Remember that really big twisty wind?

You know Mommy...remember?"...

Mommy will know that I'm not telling the truth. That will be a very big wrong thing for me to do. Wrong to break Mommy's very favorite flowers because I was playing where I was told not to. And... even more wrong would be lying to my Mommy about what happened.

That would not be honest, it would not be a nice thing for me to do to Mommy and I would not be my best *me*.

Mommy says it takes bravery sometimes to tell the truth. She says in our family we are always honest and can trust each other to tell the truth. But sometimes it can be scary to tell the truth when you know you may be in big trouble.

I decided the best thing for me to do was to tell Mommy the truth about spinning onto her very favorite flowers. I decided to be honest about what had really happened. I was hoping Mommy would not be too angry.

I was ready to be in big trouble.

I know it is always important to be honest when you do something wrong. Mommy very quietly listened to me explain what really happened to the flowers. She told me she loved me and hugged me really tight. Mommy was sad for her very favorite flowers but was really proud of my honesty for telling her the truth. I was really proud of me too.

So now Mommy says I have to make things right. It is part of growing up to be the best *me* that I can be. I know I didn't listen to Mommy. I was playing where I was told not to. It was because of what I did that Mommy's very favorite flowers got broken.

I was invited to play with my friends in the park today. Instead, Mommy says I am helping her in her garden. I am sad I'm not with my friends.

Mommy calls it *"learning the consequences"*.
Those are really big words for learning from
what happens because of what I do.

We are going to fix her flowers. I may be
sad not to be with my friends but I am happy
that I was honest and told the truth.

I am very happy that my Mommy is proud of me
and that Mommy will have new favorite flowers.

What do I know about honesty?

It means telling the truth. It means not doing what I know is wrong. It means being honest about what really happened. Telling the truth is the right thing to do even if I think I am in big trouble.

Sometimes it takes bravery to be honest...
But... honesty makes me proud of what I do and a better best *me* that I can be!

Hello Readers!

Amazon reviews can make a huge difference
to the overall success of this Book.

If you enjoyed reading this Book as much as I have enjoyed
writing it, please take a few moments to leave a quick review.

I would really appreciate it!

Thank You!

ROSE ANGEBRANDT